AMBUSH!

A Robin Hood Adventure

Jan Burchett & Sara Vogler

**FICTION
EXPRESS**

What do other readers think?

Here are some comments left on the Fiction Express blog about this book:

"Ambush *was a good book.*"
Julia, Bradford

"Thanks for the awesome story. I can't wait until the next one."
Anonymous, Ilminster

"I really enjoyed your book. The story was so good that I wanted to read it all by myself. Thanks for a great read."
Magnus, Crewe

"We love Ambush. *It is so mysterious."*
Valentina, Keighley

Contents

For Kieran Vyas, computer hero.

Love from Jan and Sara

Chapter 1

A Terrible Discovery

Sam and Kate dragged the heavy basket of logs across the great hall. The great hall was the biggest room in Nottingham Castle. It needed a very big fire. Every morning, Sam and his sister got up very early to light it.

"I hate working for the Sheriff of Nottingham," Kate groaned.

"I wish we could run away. I wish we could join Robin Hood and his men."

Robin Hood was their hero. They'd heard lots of stories about him. He lived deep in Sherwood Forest with his band of outlaws. They were thieves but they only stole from the rich. And they never kept the money. They gave it all to the poor.

"Shhh!" said Sam. He looked frightened. "Supposing the sheriff hears you."

"His face will turn purple and steam will come out of his ears," laughed Kate.

But Sam didn't laugh. "And then he'll thrash you with his stick," he said.

The door of the great hall crashed open. The Sheriff of Nottingham stormed in. His black cloak swirled round him, and his pointed nose looked even sharper in the candlelight. Sam and Kate quickly piled the logs into the grate. Had he heard them?

Then they saw the captain of the castle guards sidle in after him. He was twisting his hat nervously in his hands.

"You and your guards are fools, Captain Crabtree!" the sheriff bellowed at him. "You let Robin Hood's men beat you again."

Sam and Kate's ears pricked up.

"And you let them steal my money!" the sheriff went on.

"It wasn't our fault, sir," whimpered Crabtree. "There were lots of them. They jumped on us from the trees."

The sheriff slammed his fist down on a nearby table. "I will not stand for this any longer!" he shouted. "Now, listen carefully. I am going to set a trap for Robin Hood."

Sam and Kate looked at each other in alarm.

Chapter 2

The Sheriff's Plan

"This is my plan," said the sheriff to his captain. "I will spread the word that a rich merchant will be on the road this Wednesday night." The sheriff smiled a cold smile. "He will travel through Sherwood Forest. He will be carrying a bag of gold. Hood and his bunch of thugs will be sure to attack him."

Captain Crabtree looked puzzled. "But sir, that means Hood will have more of your money than ever."

"You brainless idiot, Crabtree!" screeched the sheriff. "There won't be any money. It's a trick. *You* will pretend to be the rich merchant and you will carry a bag of stones."

"Me, sir? But–" began Crabtree.

"Silence!" hissed the sheriff. "As soon as the outlaws jump out at you, your men will ambush them. And I will be there to see my enemy finally caught! You have two days. Now go and get ready!"

"Yes, sir. Very good, sir," said Crabtree weakly. He gave a bow and hurried out of the room.

The sheriff followed. But he whipped round at the door. His mean little eyes bored into Sam and Kate. "Do not repeat one word of what you have heard!" he snapped. "Or you will regret it."

He swept out, slamming the door as he went.

Kate grabbed her brother's arm and pulled him towards the door. "We have to get out of the castle," she said. "We must warn Robin

Hood. He's in terrible danger."

"We can't," said Sam. "Remember what happened last time we tried to run away? We'll be thrown in the dungeon again."

"Then we won't get caught this time," said Kate firmly. She led him outside.

"But the road through Sherwood Forest is so long," said Sam. "We'd never find Robin."

"We have to try," said Kate.

Sam didn't say anything for a moment. Then he nodded. "So how are we going to escape?"

Chapter 3

On the Run

"Getting out of the castle won't be easy," said Kate.

"The sheriff keeps everything locked," agreed Sam.

They peered across the courtyard at the huge castle gates. Alfred the gatekeeper was sitting on a stool. He was fast asleep.

"Now's our chance!" whispered

Kate. "We'll take his keys while he's sleeping!"

At that moment Captain Crabtree appeared. He hurried across the courtyard and gave Alfred a prod.

"Open up," he ordered. "I'm on important business."

Grumbling, Alfred took the keys from his belt. He opened a small door in one of the huge gates. Crabtree pushed past and Alfred locked it again.

"Now what?" said Kate in despair. "He's wide awake."

"I've got a plan," said Sam. He whispered in his sister's ear.

Kate rushed off. Soon she was back with a tankard of ale. She took it to Alfred.

"I thought you'd be thirsty," Kate told him. Suddenly she 'tripped'. The ale spilled all over the old man.

"Clumsy girl!" he shouted.

"Sorry," cried Kate. She dabbed the front of the gatekeeper's tunic with her apron.

Alfred's back was to the small door. Silently, Sam crept up behind him and lifted the keys off his belt.

He unlocked the door as quietly as he could.

But the key clunked in the lock.

Alfred whipped round. "What are you doing?" he demanded.

Kate dodged past him. She darted through the door after Sam. Sam slammed it shut, locked it again and threw the keys into the moat.

"That'll stop them," he said.

They raced away from the castle, glancing nervously back. But no one was following.

Chapter 4

An Unpleasant Disguise

All through a hot afternoon, they trudged up hill and down. At last they saw Sherwood Forest in the distance.

"We'll soon be there now," said Kate.

They walked past a tumbledown cottage. Pigs were snuffling about in a nearby sty.

"What do we do after we've warned Robin Hood?" said Sam. "We can't live at the castle any more and we've got no family."

"Mum used to talk about her brother, our Uncle Jonathan," said Kate. "We could try to find him and–."

"Listen," Sam interrupted her. "I can hear hoofbeats!"

"Stop!" came a shout.

Sam looked back. "A castle guard!" he said, horrified.

They dived behind the sty. They heard the guard jump off his horse.

"He'll find us!" whispered Sam.

"No, he won't," muttered Kate. "He'll find two farmhands – and both of them boys."

They climbed into the sty among the grunting pigs. Clothes had been laid to dry over a nearby bush. Kate snatched two smocks and they pulled them on. She took Sam's cap from him and stuffed her hair inside it. She stepped into a pair of damp breeches and tucked her skirt into them.

"We're too clean," said Sam.

He scooped something up from

the straw and wiped brown smears across her cheeks. "I hope this is mud," he said.

"It's not!" spluttered Kate, holding her nose.

"The sheriff himself wouldn't know us now," said Sam. He slapped smelly dung into his hair.

"The pong would keep him away!" groaned Kate.

The guard came around the cottage and up to the pigsty.

"I'm after two runaways," he growled. "Have you seen them?"

"Runaways, you say," Kate

replied, disguising her voice. "Now let me see. A boy and girl just ran by." She pointed to a track leading back to town. "They went that way… I think."

The guard stared at them for a long moment. Kate and Sam's hearts raced. At last, the man turned and stomped back to his horse.

When he was out of sight they sped for the distant trees.

They didn't stop running until they were deep in Sherwood Forest.

It was dark and creepy. The only sounds were their panting

breath and the wind whispering in the trees.

Kate shivered. "I feel as if we're being watched," she said.

"Wha– oh no!" they cried together....

Chapter 5

Captured!

Kate and Sam were suddenly knocked to the ground. They felt rough sacks being pulled over their heads. Their hands were firmly tied behind their backs.

"Let us go!" yelled Kate. She thrashed about blindly.

"Not a chance," growled a voice.

"You're coming with us," said

another, dragging them both to their feet.

They were pushed forwards and made to walk.

That guard must have gone back to the castle for help, thought Kate. Now we're for it.

Terrified, they stumbled through the undergrowth. Their feet caught on roots, and brambles scratched their legs. At last they were pulled to a halt. Their sacks were quickly whipped whipped away.

Blinking, they stared around them. A group of men in dark

green clothes sat by a blazing fire. Some were repairing bows. Others were sharpening arrows.

They all fell silent when they saw Kate and Sam.

One of the men got to his feet. He towered over them. Sam felt his heart thudding. "Who do we have here?" the man demanded. His voice was deep and commanding. "A couple of pig herders?"

"They certainly smell like them," called someone.

"They were sneaking through the forest," said one of their captors.

"Too close to the camp," said the other. "They could be spies for the sheriff."

"We're not spies!" Sam dared to say. "We hate the sheriff."

"Well said," declared a man in monk's clothing.

"So what are two children doing in Sherwood Forest?" asked the tall man. "It's a dangerous place."

Kate thought of the stories she'd heard about Robin Hood. He lived in a secret camp with his outlaws. They wore green so they wouldn't be seen among the trees. And everybody knew that one of his band was a monk.

"We were searching for Robin Hood," said Kate, staring boldly at the tall man. "And I think we've found him."

Sam's jaw dropped open. "You're Robin Hood?" he gasped, gazing up at his hero.

"I am," said Robin. He gave the order for their hands to be untied.

Chapter 6

The Merry Men
(and Woman)

Suddenly a man burst into the camp. "Welcome back, Will Scarlett," said Robin. "What news?"

"*Good* news," said Will, throwing himself down by the fire. He didn't seem to notice Kate and Sam. "A rich merchant will be travelling through the forest tomorrow night.

With a bag of gold."

"More money for the poor," said the monk, rubbing his hands.

"That's right, Friar Tuck," said Robin. "Here's the plan. He'll probably be changing horses at Hangman's Oak. We'll lie in wait there– "

"You mustn't!" cried Sam. "It's a trap."

"Who are these two ruffians?" grinned Will in surprise.

"Sam and I work at the castle," said Kate. "At least we did. But we overheard the sheriff plotting.

We escaped and came to warn Robin."

Robin Hood's dark eyes bored into them.

"Kate's telling the truth," insisted Sam.

"Kate?" Robin looked at her closely. "You're a girl?"

"A good disguise," said one of the outlaws. He pulled off his hat. Long hair tumbled out. "Like mine."

"Maid Marion!" gasped Sam. "We've heard how you ran away to join Robin and his men."

"That's so brave," said Kate.

"Not as brave as you two," said Marion. "You escaped from Nottingham Castle and the sheriff."

"That was brave indeed," said Robin. "Tell me what you know."

Kate and Sam told him everything they'd heard the sheriff say.

"Thank you," said Robin, when they'd finished. He took their hands in a warm grasp. "You've faced many dangers in order to help me. And now I must change my plan."

"You'll stay safe in the camp?" said Sam hopefully.

"Certainly not," replied Robin. His eyes twinkled. "The sheriff's out to trap me. Who am I to disappoint him?"

Kate and Sam were horrified.

"You can't let yourself be caught," cried Kate. "Everyone knows the sheriff wants you dead."

"Don't worry," said Marion. "Robin won't get caught."

"Can we stay and help?" Sam burst out.

Robin Hood thought for a moment. Kate and Sam held their breath. Then the outlaw grinned.

"What do you think?" he cried to his men (and woman). "Shall we see if they can pass the test?"

"Aye!" Robin's band all agreed.

Chapter 7

The Ambush

Robin Hood led Kate and Sam to a river.

"Fetch cones from that tree," he said, pointing across the fast-flowing water.

"There's no bridge," said Kate. "Just slippery rocks."

Sam's eyes brightened. "Can I borrow a long rope and a bow

and arrow?" he asked.

Marion handed them over. Sam tied the rope to the arrow. He tried to pull back the bowstring.

Will Scarlett laughed. "You're doing it wrong."

"I bet you can't hit that tree," said Sam.

"Just you watch this!" said Will.

The arrow sped across the river, the rope snaking behind. It fixed itself in the trunk.

"Thank you," said Sam, tying the other end of the rope tightly around a nearby tree. Using the rocks as stepping stones, he and Kate began to cross, clutching the rope as the water swirled at their feet. Sam's foot slipped and he fell to his knees. Kate hauled him back up. At last they reached the bank.

They plucked two cones. The outlaws cheered.

"Well done," said Robin when they'd got back. "Brave, and cunning too! Tomorrow night you'll be look-outs."

Kate and Sam glowed with pride.

"There's one more task," said Friar Tuck.

"What's that?" asked Kate, worried.

"Change your clothes!" laughed the friar, holding his nose. "You still smell like a pigsty!"

* * *

The next day they searched for fruits, gathered firewood and trimmed feathers for arrows. Will Scarlet taught them the birdcalls the outlaws used as signals.

At last Robin looked up at the darkening sky. "Time to leave," he said. "The moon will light our way."

The outlaws slung their bows over their shoulders.

Sam's heart raced at the thought of the adventure to come.

Will Scarlet pulled at a creeper hanging from a tree. Kate's jaw dropped as a rope ladder unrolled.

"It's our secret way through the forest," said Marion. "Follow me."

At the top, ropes criss-crossed amongst the trees.

Chapter 8

On the Look-Out

Kate and Sam swung from branch to branch with the outlaws. They came to a rope walkway high among the leaves. It led to a stout tree.

"Hangman's Oak," hissed Robin.

One by one the outlaws dropped silently down from the trees and disappeared. Only Maid Marion was left.

"This is your look-out spot," she whispered. "That branch above the road. Give your signal when the merchant appears." Then she, too, was gone.

Kate and Sam hid themselves among the leaves.

The empty road stretched away. They waited, not daring to move. "What was that?" whispered Kate.

Someone was riding slowly along. He held a lantern. He looked like a rich merchant. He also looked like a very nervous Captain Crabtree.

Kate gave three owl hoots.

Robin Hood swung down and landed in front of the horse.

"What have we he–" before he could finish, a group of guards burst out from the trees. The outlaw struggled but they soon had him tied up.

A rider in black came galloping up. It was the Sheriff of Nottingham. He poked the prisoner with his sword. "Looks as if your 'merry' men have deserted you, Hood!" sniggered the sheriff. The prisoner silently bent his head. "You're at my mercy. To the castle! Walk!"

Keeping out of sight, Kate and

Sam tailed them down the long road to Nottingham.

* * *

The sheriff's men reached the castle walls as dawn broke.

"Lower the drawbridge!" ordered the sheriff.

Nothing happened. The guards rushed forward, puzzled.

Kate took her chance. She crept up behind the prisoner and undid his bound hands.

Then she gasped as a tall figure appeared on the battlements.

"Robin Hood!" blustered the sheriff. "Then who–"

The freed prisoner threw off his cap. Long hair tumbled out.

"Maid Marion!" exclaimed Kate.

Marion winked at Kate. Then she leapt at the sheriff and snatched his sword.

"You tricked me, Hood!" bellowed the sheriff.

"You left the place unguarded," called Robin. His outlaws appeared beside him. "We've helped ourselves to a few things. So here's a gift in return."

Chapter 9

Robin's Revenge

Robin aimed an arrow from the castle battlements. It sped through the air and hit the sheriff's shield right in the centre. The sheriff gave a yelp. His horse neighed in terror. It kicked up its back legs and the sheriff went sailing over its head. Splash! He landed in the smelly moat.

"To the forest!" yelled Robin.

The outlaws raced from the ramparts. They let the drawbridge down and charged across it. The guards surged towards them, waving their weapons. Robin Hood and his men leapt on them.

Marion turned the sheriff's sword on Captain Crabtree. "Tell your men to surrender!" she ordered him.

But Crabtree just quivered with fright. "Help!" he squeaked.

Three guards broke away from the fight and rushed to rescue their captain.

"Oh, no you don't!" muttered Sam. He picked up the rope that had bound Marion's hands. He held one end and Kate held the other. Hiding from view they stretched it across the guards' path. The guards didn't see the rope. They fell in a tangle of chainmail and swords.

"Well done!" called Robin. He was fighting two men at once but he still had time to touch his cap to them.

Kate saw a guard creeping up on Will Scarlett. "Look out, Will!" she cried.

Will whipped round. The guard's sword thudded against his stick. He pushed Will backwards.

The sheriff was clambering up the slippery bank. He had a fish stuck in his hat and he was dripping with pondweed. "Finish him off!" he screeched to the guard.

But Kate wasn't going to let that happen. She crept up behind the guard and tapped him on the back. "Excuse me," she said politely. The guard turned. Will whacked him over the head with his stick.

The guard went stumbling away.

He crashed into the sheriff. The sheriff fell back into the water again.

Friar Tuck came over the drawbridge. He was leading some horses.

"Time to go," called Robin. He swung into a saddle. "You're with me," he said, hauling Sam up behind him.

Marion booted Captain Crabtree into the moat beside his master. "Ride with me, Kate," she cried.

The outlaws galloped away from Nottingham Castle.

Chapter 10

A Nice Surprise

"The sheriff was very generous with his gold," laughed Robin as they all sat round the fire back at their camp. He scooped out a fistful of coins from an open chest. "We'll share this among the good people of Nottingham."

"And he was very generous with his food," said Friar Tuck, chewing a chicken bone.

Sam turned to his sister. "Do ou think we can stay with the outlaws?" he whispered.

"I hope so," Kate replied.

"Have I missed a raid?" bellowed a loud voice.

A newcomer strode into the camp. He was dressed like the outlaws. If Kate and Sam had thought Robin was tall, this man was a giant.

"Little John!" called Robin. "You're just in time. The sheriff has provided us with a feast."

"Splendid!" Little John rubbed his hands together. Then he spotted

Kate and Sam and stopped in surprise. "Who have we got here?"

"New recruits," said Robin, slapping them both on the back. "And brave with it."

Kate squeezed Sam's hand. Robin must mean that they could stay.

"Where have you two come from?" asked Little John. He peered from one to the other. He had a strange look on his face.

Kate told him that they'd lived at Nottingham Castle for almost as long as they could remember.

"Would you be called Katherine

and Samuel, by any chance?" Little John seemed very keen to know the answer.

Kate and Sam nodded, wondering how he knew their names.

"Have you any relatives?" said Little John.

"We have an Uncle Jonathan somewhere," said Sam. "But we don't know where he is or what he looks li–"

"*I* am your Uncle Jonathan!" declared Little John. "I've been searching for you for years."

Kate and Sam were stunned.

For so long they'd dreamed of having a home and a family. Now they had both!

Little John held out his arms. They ran to him.

The outlaws gave a rousing cheer.

Friar Tuck chuckled. "That's what I call a happy ending."

THE END

FICTION EXPRESS

THE READERS TAKE CONTROL!

Have you ever wanted to change the course of a plot, change a character's destiny, tell an author what to write next?

Well, now you can!

'Ambush!' was originally written for the award-winning interactive e-book website Fiction Express.

Fiction Express e-books are published in gripping weekly episodes. At the end of each episode, readers are given voting options to decide where the plot goes next. They vote online and the winning vote is then conveyed to the author who writes the next episode, in real time, according to the readers' most popular choice.

www.fictionexpress.co.uk

WINNER
Education Resources
Award for Innovation

FICTION EXPRESS

TALK TO THE AUTHORS

The Fiction Express website features a blog where readers can interact with the authors while they are writing. An exciting and unique opportunity!

FANTASTIC TEACHER RESOURCES

Each weekly Fiction Express episode comes with a PDF of teacher resources packed with ideas to extend the text.

"The teaching resources are fab and easily fill a whole week of literacy lessons!"
Rachel Humphries, teacher at Westacre Middle School

FICTI💬N EXPRESS

Deena's Dreadful Day
by Simon Cheshire

Deena is preparing for her big moment – a part in the local talent contest – but everything is going wrong. Her mum and dad are no help, and only her dog, Bert, seems to understand.

Will Deena and Bert make it to the theatre in time? Will her magic tricks work or will her dreadful day end in disaster?

ISBN 978-1-78322-569-9

FICTI😮N EXPRESS

Emery the Explorer: A Jungle Adventure
by Louise John

When the postman delivers half of a mysterious treasure map through Emery's letterbox, the young explorer knows that a new adventure is about to begin. The trail leads him and his pet monkey, Spider, deep into the steamy Amazon jungle.

Can Emery survive the dangers of the rain forest? Will he succeed in finding the treasure before Dex D Saster, his biggest rival, or will his jungle adventure end in failure?

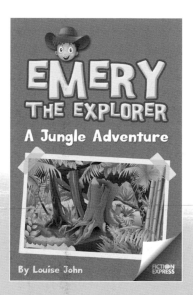

ISBN 978-1-78322-570-5

FICTI●N EXPRESS

The House on Strange Street
by Simon Cheshire

Dad wants to buy the rundown house on Strange Street, but Joel and Zoe aren't so sure. The garden is overgrown, the paint is flaking off the windows and the roof leaks. Inside, the place is very dusty, creepy and spooky. It's full of weird noises and creaking floorboards, and... what was that? A shadow? Or was it some kind of scary creature?

Should the family risk it, and buy the house or get out of there as fast as they can?

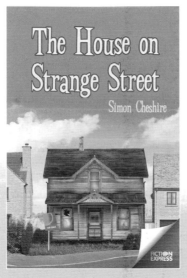

ISBN 978-1-78322-580-4

FICTI🗨N EXPRESS

The Sand Witch
by Tommy Donbavand

When twins Chris and Ella are left to look after their younger brother on a deserted beach, they expect everything to be normal, boring in fact. But then something extraordinary happens! Will the Sand Witch succeed in passing on her sandy curse in this exciting adventure?

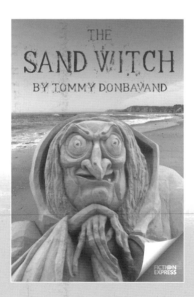

ISBN 978-1-78322-544-6

Snaffles the Cat Burglar
by Cavan Scott

When notorious feline felon Snaffles and his dim canine sidekick Bonehead are caught red-pawed trying to steal the Sensational Salmon of Sumatra, not everything is what it seems. Their capture leads them on a top-secret mission for the Ministry of Secret Shenanigans.

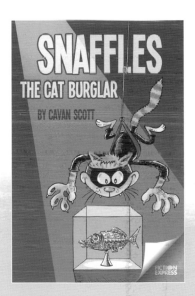

ISBN 978-1-78322-543-9

About the Authors

Sara Vogler (left) and Jan Burchett (right) were already friends when they discovered they both wanted to write children's books and that it was much more fun to do it together. In between the cups of tea and gossip they have managed to produce over 170 books. These are wide-ranging and include stories about ghosts, football, ghosts playing football, Tudor detectives, dinosaurs, pets from space and time-travelling pirates. Jan lives in Essex and Sara lives in London, and are both owned by black cats who rule their households.